Gooney Bird on the Map

by
LOIS LOWRY

Illustrated by Middy Thomas

Houghton Mifflin Books for Children
HOUGHTON MIFFLIN HARCOURT
Boston   New York

To Hannah, Rorry, and Jax

Text copyright © 2011 by Lois Lowry

Illustrations copyright © 2011 by Middy Thomas

Houghton Mifflin Books for Children is an imprint of Houghton Mifflin Harcourt Publishing Company.

www.hmhbooks.com

The text of this book is set in Garamond MT.

Library of Congress Cataloging-in-Publication Control Number 2011012160

ISBN 978-0-547-55622-2

Manufactured in the United States of America

EB 10 9 8 7

4500404979

1.

"February vacation soon, students! Just ten more days!" Mr. Leroy, the school principal, pointed out, after he had made his usual announcements on the intercom. "I hope all of you have wonderful plans!"

The second-graders wiggled in their seats and began to murmur. *Vacation, vacation, vacation.* Even though they loved school, vacations were always exciting. "I'm going to—" Ben began.

"My family's—" Barry Tuckerman whispered loudly.

But Mrs. Pidgeon put her finger to her

mouth and reminded them that the announcements weren't finished. "Shhh," she said.

"And we mustn't forget," Mr. Leroy continued, "that this month we are celebrating the birthdays of two of our most important presidents. Let's finish up this morning's announcements by singing to them, shall we?"

Mr. Leroy started off. "Happy birthday to youuuuu," he sang. In every classroom in the Watertower Elementary School, the students joined in. Some of them sang, "Dear Abe," some sang, "Dear George," and some tried to fit in "Dear Abraham-and-George."

Gooney Bird Greene, at her desk in Mrs. Pidgeon's classroom, sang loudly, "Dear George-Abraham-William-Henry-and-Ronald." She was still singing the list of names after the others had finished the last "Happy birthday to you." So she sang her own final line all by herself. The other children all stared at her.

But Gooney Bird didn't mind. "I am never ever embarrassed," she had once said. And that

3

seemed to be true. Now, after she concluded, "Happy birthday to you," she folded her hands on her desk, looked up toward the front of the room, and cheerfully waited for the school day to begin.

"Goodness," Mrs. Pidgeon said. "Who were all of those people, Gooney Bird?"

"Presidents with February birthdays," Gooney Bird explained. "I don't think it's fair that George Washington and Abraham Lincoln get all the attention."

"But they were important guys!" Barry Tuckerman pointed out.

"All presidents are important," Gooney Bird said.

"I don't even know who those other ones are," Chelsea said.

"Well, let's find out," Mrs. Pidgeon said. She began writing on the board. "George. Abraham. And who were the others, Gooney Bird?"

"William-Henry-Ronald."

Mrs. Pidgeon wrote those names on the board. "All right, class. Who was George?"

"Washington!" the children called, and Mrs. Pidgeon wrote "Washington" on the board after "George."

"Abraham?" she asked, and the children all said, "Lincoln!" So she wrote that.

"William?" she asked, but the room was silent. "Well, it could be Bill Clinton, I suppose," she said. "But President Taft was also named William, and—oh, dear. There might be *lots* of Williams . . ."

At her desk, Gooney Bird sighed loudly.

"Henry? Anyone know Henry?" Mrs. Pidgeon left "William" blank and held her chalk beside Henry's name. Gooney Bird sighed again.

She left "Henry" blank. "Ronald?" Mrs. Pidgeon said. "Oh, I know that one, for sure!" She wrote "Reagan" after "Ronald." "I remember when he was president. It wasn't that long ago. But William and Henry? Help me out here, Gooney Bird."

"Actually," Gooney Bird explained, "it wasn't *William, comma, Henry, comma, Ronald.* It was *William Henry, comma,* and *Ronald.* Ronald Reagan, just like you said. And William Henry Harrison.

"I kind of like when people have two first names, don't you?" asked Gooney Bird. "It makes them somewhat special, don't you think?"

Felicia Ann, at her desk, nodded her head. The other children frowned a bit.

"William Henry Harrison was born in February," Gooney Bird went on. "He was president of the United States, but only for one month."

"How come? Everybody gets to be president for four years! We learned that!" Malcolm was partway out of his desk. "Four years! Right, Mrs. Pidgeon? Didn't we learn that? Four years?"

The teacher gently placed her calm-down

hand on Malcolm's shoulder. "Gooney Bird?" she said. "Want to explain?"

"He died. Moment of silence, please."

"Moment of silence?" Mrs. Pidgeon repeated with a questioning look.

"When you hear something sad and serious," Gooney Bird explained, "you should always have a moment of silence. You don't have to close your eyes or anything."

"Well, I like the idea of an occasional moment of silence," Mrs. Pidgeon said. "Let's do it. A moment of silence for William Henry Harrison, class, because he died after being president for only one month."

"Bummer!" said Tyrone. He began one of his raps. *First he be elected, then he be rejected . . ."*

"Moment of silence, Tyrone," Gooney Bird reminded him. "Anyway, he wasn't rejected," she pointed out. "He got sick and died."

The class was all silent for a few seconds.

"And nobody remembers him," Keiko added, sadly.

"Except Gooney Bird Greene," Nicholas pointed out.

"I remember *everything*," Gooney Bird said.

"Well," Mrs. Pidgeon said, after the moment of silence had ended and she had looked around the room with a sigh, "another day in the second grade. I wish we had cleaned this mess up better yesterday before school ended."

The children all agreed. They had been working on valentines to take home to their parents. Now the valentines were done, but there was red construction paper everywhere, as well as scissors and paste, Magic Markers, and white paper that they had folded and cut into snowflakes. Tiny white scraps were all over the floor.

"Mr. Furillo will clean it up," Nicholas said. "That's his job."

"Nope," the teacher said. "It's our job. Let's do it quickly. We have to get to work on our geography lesson."

"Mrs. Pidgeon?" Gooney Bird raised her hand. "I have an idea! We could do both at once!"

"Sounds good." Mrs. Pidgeon had begun to walk around the room, collecting unused sheets of construction paper. She held a stack of red papers in her hand. When she got to Gooney Bird's desk she looked down in surprise. "My goodness!" she said. "A *blue* valentine?"

Gooney Bird nodded. She looked proudly at the large blue paper heart that she had decorated with a yellow arrow, and the words I LOVE YOU carefully lettered in brown. "Yes," she said. "I like to be different."

Mrs. Pidgeon looked at Gooney Bird, who today was wearing unmatched socks, knickers, and a pearl necklace over her LOVE YOUR MOTHER T-shirt. "I know you do," she said fondly. "Finished with your paste?"

Gooney Bird nodded, and Mrs. Pidgeon picked up the square of paper with a white dab of dried paste on it. "Here's what we'll do," she announced to the class. "Put your valentines away neatly in your desks so they don't get crumpled. I'll come around with the wastebasket, and each of you deposit all of your used paste and your paper scraps."

"Like on an airplane!" Barry announced. "When the flight attendant comes around with a plastic trash bag!"

"Yes, a little like that," Mrs. Pidgeon said. She went to the front of the room and picked up the large wastebasket.

"I'm going on an airplane for vacation! I'm going all the way to—"

"Enough, Barry! We've all heard about your plans."

"Me too!" Beanie called out. "I'm going on a plane!"

Hastily Mrs. Pidgeon set the wastebasket down, went to the piano, and played a chord to quiet the class. Then she played the opening line to a familiar song, a song that the children had sung many times.

" 'This Land Is Your Land'!" Chelsea called.

"Right," Mrs. Pidgeon said. She stood up and started around with the wastebasket. "This land is our land, and we're going to work again today on the state capitals."

"Tyrone can't use his lunch box!" Malcolm called. "No fair for him to use his lunch box!"

"No, Tyrone won't use his lunch box. It's in your cubby, isn't it, Tyrone?"

Tyrone nodded. All of the children looked toward Tyrone's cubby. They could see the handle of his lunch box poking out below his hat and mittens. Tyrone's lunch box listed all the states, their capitals, and the names of famous people who had been born there.

"All right, here we go! You all should be cleaning up your valentine scraps! First state: Massachusetts!"

"Boston!" the children called.

"Correct." Mrs. Pidgeon stopped at Malcolm's desk and helped him put his valentines neatly away. He had made three red decorated hearts for the triplet babies at home. As always, his desk was a mess, but with Mrs. Pidgeon's help he tidied things up. He leaned down and picked up some scraps from the floor and dropped them in the basket.

"Good job, Malcolm. Class? Next state: Colorado!"

"Denver!" the second-graders shouted.

"That was easy!" Chelsea pointed out. "Give us a hard one!"

"Okay," said Mrs. Pidgeon. She held the wastebasket, and Keiko carefully swept her scraps into it from her desktop with the side of her hand. "Michigan!"

No one said anything. Finally, Felicia Ann remembered Michigan's capital. "Lansing!" she called, and everyone cheered.

"How come you didn't get it, Gooney Bird? I thought you remember *everything!*" Tyrone asked.

"I was thinking about something else," Gooney Bird explained. "My mind was elsewhere. I'm beginning to get a really good idea. But it's only in teeny pieces so far. I have to put it together in my mind."

"Cool," Tyrone said.

"Speaking of cool, how about this one? Vermont!" Mrs. Pidgeon announced.

After a moment, the children responded, "Montpelier!"

"Hey, did I tell you? I'm going to Sugarbush, Vermont, for vacation!" Ben called. "And I'm taking snowboard lessons! And we're staying in a hotel and—"

"You told us a thousand times," Malcolm muttered.

"A million times," Chelsea said.

Mrs. Pidgeon interrupted. "Next: Florida!"

"Orlando!" called Beanie.

"Nope, dummy! It's Tallahassee!" Barry corrected her.

"Yes, Tallahassee!" the other children agreed.

Beanie giggled. "I knew that! I just wanted

to say Orlando because that's where my family's going on vacation! Disney World! We're flying to Orlando, and our hotel has a swimming pool, and I have a new bathing suit, and—"

"Big deal!" called Barry. "*I'm* going to Hawaii and—"

"Poor William Henry Harrison never once went to Disney World," Gooney Bird announced in a loud, mournful voice. "Moment of silence."

The class fell silent in sympathy for President Harrison, and Mrs. Pidgeon returned the wastebasket to its spot near the door.

2.

"My lunch is somewhat dull today," commented Gooney Bird as she unwrapped a sandwich later that morning. "I wish I had a kumquat."

"Your lunch is never dull," Mrs. Pidgeon said, looking over from her desk. "What's in that sandwich?"

Most of the teachers ate their lunch in the teachers' lounge, but Mrs. Pidgeon usually sat with the children. She had confided in them, "Don't tell anyone I said this, but your conversation is more interesting. And I hate watching people eat microwaved soup."

Gooney Bird pried up one corner of the bread and examined her sandwich. "Spinach," she said. "Crumbled bacon. Gorgonzola cheese. And some chopped walnuts."

"There you go," said the teacher. "Most interesting lunch in town. And look here, everyone. I've brought a surprise for dessert." She set a small paper bag on her desk.

"What is it?" asked Chelsea.

"Candy hearts," Mrs. Pidgeon explained. "We've been busy making valentines for our families but we didn't have anything really special for ourselves."

"Do they have sayings on them?" Chelsea asked, leaning forward to try to peek into the bag.

"Yes. The standard valentine-heart sayings."

"How about if we each take one, and then we can see what they say, but we promise not to eat them till after we finish our lunch?" Malcolm suggested.

Mrs. Pidegon laughed. Sometimes she called Malcolm Mr. Eager.

"Okay," she told them. She passed the bag around and each child took a candy heart.

"Oops!" Gooney Bird said in a dismayed voice. "Mine says *Kiss Me*!"

"That's okay, Gooney Bird," Tricia reassured her. "Valentines always say romantic things. See mine? It says *Pucker Up*."

"Yes, but remember my sandwich?" Gooney Bird asked. "Gorgonzola. It's really stinky. Kissing me would be gross. I'm trading *Kiss Me* in for a different one." She reached into the bag a second time, and smiled when she read her new candy heart. "*Très Chic*. That's better!"

"What's 'Tray Sheek'?" Nicholas asked.

"It means 'fashionable' in French," Mrs. Pidgeon explained. "Just right for Gooney Bird, I think."

The other children looked at Gooney Bird, and nodded in agreement. In addition to her

mismatched socks, she was wearing green nail polish today. *"Très Chic,"* Keiko murmured in admiration.

"I don't get my heart," Chelsea complained, squinting at the candy in her hand. "It says something about a quart."

"Let's see," Mrs. Pidgeon said. She looked carefully at the saying and then smiled. *"URA QT,"* she read. "'You are a cutie'! And that's true, Chelsea."

Chelsea grinned. "I'm a cutie. A QT!" she said.

"Mine says *Magic,"* said Nicholas. "You think it means Magic Johnson?"

"Nope," Gooney Bird told him. "It just means you are magical. What's yours, Barry?"

Barry Tuckerman had been carefully un-wrapping a sandwich that was neatly cut into four triangles. He wrinkled his nose a bit. "Tuna fish," he said. "Anyone want to trade?"

But no one wanted tuna fish. Barry shrugged and took a bite.

But no one wanted tuna fish. Barry shrugged and took a bite.

"I meant: what's the saying on your heart?"

Barry picked up his candy heart and examined it. *"Whiz Kid,"* he read. Everyone laughed. The heart seemed to describe Barry very well.

After a moment he asked, "How many days till the start of vacation? I forget what Mr. Leroy said."

"Well," Mrs. Pidgeon told him. "Vacation begins on the seventeenth, and today is the seventh. Seventeen minus seven?"

"Mrs. Pidgeon," Keiko said with a grin, "you always try to sneak math problems into everything."

"Ten!" Barry said. "And in ten days this Whiz Kid is going to be eating coconuts and pineapples, and sandwiches with little paper parasols stuck in them."

"How come?" asked Tricia, with her mouth full.

"Remember? We're going to Hawaii for winter vacation."

"You goin' to be dancin' the hula, *Whiz Kid*!" Tyrone said. He stood and wiggled his hips. Then he examined his own candy heart. "*Cool Dude*!" he read. "YES!"

"And look! My heart says *Sunshine*!" Beanie told everyone. "Just right for someone who's going to Disney World!"

"We're going to go skiing with my cousins, in Sugarbush, Vermont!" Ben said.

"We know that already, Ben," Malcolm said loudly. "You've told us that a gazillion times."

Ben ignored him. He read his heart and made a face. "*In Style*. Well, I guess that's true," he said. "I have a new snowboard."

"You gonna freeze," Tyrone told him. "It's about a hundred degrees below zero in Vermont. And Barry? You gonna roast, in Hawaii. You better take a gallon of sunscreen, *Whiz Kid*."

"And sunglasses!" Malcolm said. He held two Oreos over his eyes, like dark lenses.

"What's your heart, Malcolm?" Tyrone asked. "Cuz I'm *Cool Dude*. What're you?"

Malcolm looked for his heart. The space in front of him was, like Malcolm himself, very disorganized. Half of his sandwich was un-eaten and soggy with spilled milk. Finally, under a crumpled, wet napkin, he found his heart and read it aloud. *"Class Act."* Everyone hooted with laughter. Malcolm grinned. *"Class Act,* that's me!" he said proudly.

"Mrs. Pidgeon?" Felicia Ann asked suddenly, in her quiet voice. Everyone smiled. Felicia Ann's two front teeth had come in at last, and she no longer said "Mittheth Pidgeon."

"Yes?"

"What's Up? That's my heart: a question."

"Well, that's wonderful! I love it when students have questions!"

"And I have a question right now," Felicia Ann said. "Why is it hot in one place and cold in another, when it's February in both places?"

"Yeah!" said Tyrone. "Makes no sense!"

"Yes, what's up with that?" asked studious Barry, frowning.

"Well," said Mrs. Pidgeon. She picked up Keiko's orange. "May I borrow this for a minute?" she asked.

Keiko nodded. "I'm *Sweet Thing*," she said, holding up her heart.

"You are indeed, Keiko. Now, class: picture a line around it, exactly in the middle," Mrs. Pidgeon suggested. With her finger she traced an imaginary line around the orange.

"Like an obi?" Keiko said. "Around my *obaachan*'s middle?" When she saw that the children looked puzzled, she explained, "That means 'grandma.' When my *obaachan* wears a kimono, she has an obi tied around—"

"Oh, Keiko, I'm sorry," Mrs. Pidgeon said. "I should have explained that I meant the orange to be the *earth*."

"Like Gooney Bird's LOVE YOUR MOTHER T-shirt, with the picture of the earth on it?" Keiko asked.

"Just like that," the teacher said with a smile.

"What line goes around the middle of the earth?" she asked.

Malcolm leaped from his chair. "I know! I know! The equator!" he shouted.

The other children all nodded, remembering. "Equator," they said. "Equator."

"Right! And the closer you are to the equator, the warmer it will be. Hawaii is closer to the equator than Vermont. So Hawaii—"

"—is very, very warm," Barry pointed out. "That's why I'll be surfing, and people in Vermont will be—"

"Snowboarding!" Ben said. "Which is way cooler than lying on a beach!"

"Excuse me," Beanie announced, "but in Orlando, Florida, where I will just happen to be on my vacation, the weather will be—"

Mrs. Pidgeon sighed. "Thanks, Keiko," she said, and gave the orange back.

Beanie, Ben, and Barry continued to argue

Mrs. Pidgeon sighed. "Thanks, Keiko," she said, and gave the orange back.

Beanie, Ben, and Barry continued to argue over who was going to the best vacation spot. The other children were all silent.

"Could William Henry Harrison snowboard?" Malcolm asked Gooney Bird. She shook her head no.

"Or surf?" asked Nicholas.

Gooney Bird shook her head again. "No," she said. "I think on vacations he just stayed home and had nice times with his family. Probably he went to the library."

"Or bowling," Chelsea suggested.

"I bet he played Scrabble," Felicia Ann suggested.

"Those are all good things to do on vacation," Keiko said in a small voice.

Mrs. Pidgeon folded her paper napkin and gathered her trash. "Yes," she said. "They certainly are." She leaned back in her chair and tossed her lunch remains into the trash can.

"Good shot," said Nicholas.

"Well, of course! My heart said, *U Go, Girl*," Mrs. Pidgeon pointed out.

"Everybody finished with lunch?" she asked the students. They nodded.

"And dessert? Did you eat your candy hearts?"

But the children shook their heads. They had all saved their valentine hearts carefully.

"Okay, then, I'll save mine, too," said Mrs. Pidgeon. She put her heart into the pocket of her jacket. "And now," she told them, "I'll pull down the map of the United States, and—"

"We didn't finish our math worksheets yesterday," Chelsea pointed out. "Subtraction. If one person has sixteen candy hearts and another person is very grabby and grabs five candy hearts— "

"Yes, or one person has fifty-three Oreos?" Nicholas suggested. "And then— "

"Who would have fifty-three Oreos?" Tyrone interrupted. "Nobody!" Nicholas punched him.

"Children, children, children," Mrs. Pidgeon said. She moved between the two boys and separated them.

"You said we had to have our worksheets done by the end of school yesterday," Chelsea pointed out.

Mrs. Pidgeon sighed. "Well, that's true. I did. Maybe—" she said.

"Mrs. Pidgeon?" It was Gooney Bird.

"Yes?"

"Remember I had an idea starting, and it was just in small pieces? Well, I've put it together. It's a completely ready idea now."

The second-graders all grinned with excitement. They always did when Gooney Bird had an idea.

3.

"In a minute," Gooney Bird said. "I'll tell you my idea in a minute, after Mrs. Pidgeon finishes explaining about the equator."

Several pull-down maps were rolled tight at the top of the chalkboard. "There are six maps here," Mrs. Pidgeon said. "But I'm just pulling down one at the moment. How many maps are still rolled up?"

The children groaned. "Five! That's so *easy!*" Nicholas called.

"Correct. Six minus one equals five." The teacher pulled down a map that showed the entire world, even Antarctica (Barry Tuckerman always liked to point out Antarctica). Once, Keiko had gone to this map with the pointer and shown the class Yokohama, the city in Japan that had at one time been her grandparents' home.

They all knew how to find Italy, which was easy because it was shaped like a boot. And they had found Australia on the map when they had been talking about koala bears and kangaroos not long before.

They could also find all of those things on the round globe that sat on top of the bookcase, near the hamster cage. But the pulled-down map was easier for the class to see. Now the children sat at their desks and looked carefully when Mrs. Pidgeon aimed the tip of the pointer at a faint line across the center of the map. As she moved it slowly back and forth, they could see that the line went all the way across, even through the blue of the oceans.

"Equator!" called out Barry Tuckerman.

"Correct, *Whiz Kid*!" said Mrs. Pidgeon.

"It goes through Africa!" Ben pointed out.

"And South America!" Tricia said loudly.

"How come the USA doesn't get any piece of equator?" Tyrone grumbled. "No fair."

"Well, the United States has a lot of other good things," Mrs. Pidgeon pointed out.

"Yeah, it has Disney World!" Beanie said happily.

"You'll have to wear dumb mouse ears," Malcolm said, but Beanie only grinned.

"And it has Sugarbush, Vermont!" added Ben.

"You'll freeze," Malcolm told him. "You'll get frostbite and your toes will turn black." But Ben just laughed.

"It has Hawaii!" Barry Tuckerman shouted. "Fiftieth state in the United States! Capital: Honolulu! Wait'll you see pictures of me surfing!"

"A shark will probably eat you," Malcolm said gloomily. "Or at least bite a leg off."

"Goodness, Malcolm, what's wrong? Why are you so gloomy? Aren't you looking forward to vacation?" asked Mrs. Pidgeon.

"No. We can't go anyplace because of the babies. Hey, I have an easy math problem. What if there are six people in a family, and three of them disappear?"

Everyone groaned. The baby triplets at Malcolm's house did make life difficult for his family.

"Maybe you could go to the park," Keiko suggested. "I know your mom has that huge stroller."

"In February?" Malcolm asked. "The park in *February?*"

"Well, maybe not," Keiko acknowledged.

"Announcement!" said Gooney Bird loudly. She stood up. Everyone listened.

"We all feel sorry for Malcolm because of those babies. But William Henry Harrison and his wife had ten children," Gooney Bird told the class in a serious voice. "That's spelled T-E-N. *Ten.* Moment of silence."

The room was very still. Malcolm's expression brightened a little. The announcement had made him feel a little better.

Mrs. Pidgeon let the world map go and it rolled itself up with a snap. Next she pulled down the map of the United States.

"Well," she said, "I just wanted to point out how far different places are from the equator and why some are colder than others. You see that there are other lines across the map? Those are the latitude lines. Let's find Vermont, where Ben is going skiing on vacation."

"Snowboarding," Ben corrected her.

"It's up here, in the northeast United States." She pointed. Then she leaned forward and looked carefully. "The equator is zero degrees and Vermont is about forty-four degrees north of the equator.

"Now let's find Hawaii, where Barry will be swimming."

"Surfing!" said Barry loudly.

Mrs. Pidgeon sighed. "Anyway, it's way over

here to the west. See, beyond California, out in the Pacific Ocean?" She pointed and looked closely again. "Looks as if Hawaii is about eighteen degrees above the equator. Which is farther from zero, class: forty-four or eighteen?"

"Forty-four," everyone agreed.

"My dad is forty-four," Malcolm announced.

"My mom is thirty-four," said Tricia.

"My mom is—" Felicia Ann began.

"Class?" said Mrs. Pidgeon. "You're right that forty-four is much farther from zero than eighteen. I wonder how much farther! I have a feeling we might have a math problem here. We need to do some subtraction!"

"My mom says that when she's forty she's not going to tell anybody," Chelsea announced. "She's going to be thirty-nine forever!"

"Forty minus thirty-nine equals one," Barry Tuckerman pointed out.

"But what about her driver's license?" Tyrone said. "It'll say forty on her driver's license! You can't lie to the po-leece!"

Mrs. Pidgeon took a deep breath. "Let's think about the number forty-four, class," she said. "It would be how many tens, and how many ones?"

"Lie to the cops and they bust you in the chops," Tyrone chanted.

"Bust you in the chops!" the other children echoed. Malcolm stood and began to dance. Ben threw a fake punch at Nicholas.

Mrs. Pidgeon put down the pointer. She pulled the little string that made the map recurl itself. She looked frustrated. "In your seats with your hands folded, please!" She said loudly. "Right this minute!" The children obeyed quickly.

"I didn't get to see how far Disney World is from the equator!" muttered Beanie.

"Everybody!" It was Gooney Bird's voice. She raised her hand, and Mrs. Pidgeon nodded at her.

"Is it time for your idea, Gooney Bird?" asked Felicia Ann.

"Yes," Gooney Bird said.

The children waited and listened.

"But first I have to get permission from the principal," Gooney Bird said. "Mrs. Pidgeon, is it okay if I go see Mr. Leroy for a minute?"

Mrs. Pidgeon nodded. "Yes, but if I were you, I think I'd take off the tiara. I don't think Mr. Leroy has ever fully understood your sense of style the way the rest of us do."

"I agree." Gooney Bird reached up and removed the tiara from her red hair. "Anyway, it's a good plan to look businesslike when you are conducting business. I'm going to wear gloves. I always wear gloves for serious meetings."

She went to her cubby, stored her tiara there, and pulled on a pair of white gloves that had been folded on the shelf.

The children didn't think her appearance unusual. It was just typical Gooney Bird, and they were used to it.

She stopped at the door of the classroom and smoothed the fingers of her gloves. "How do I look?" she asked.

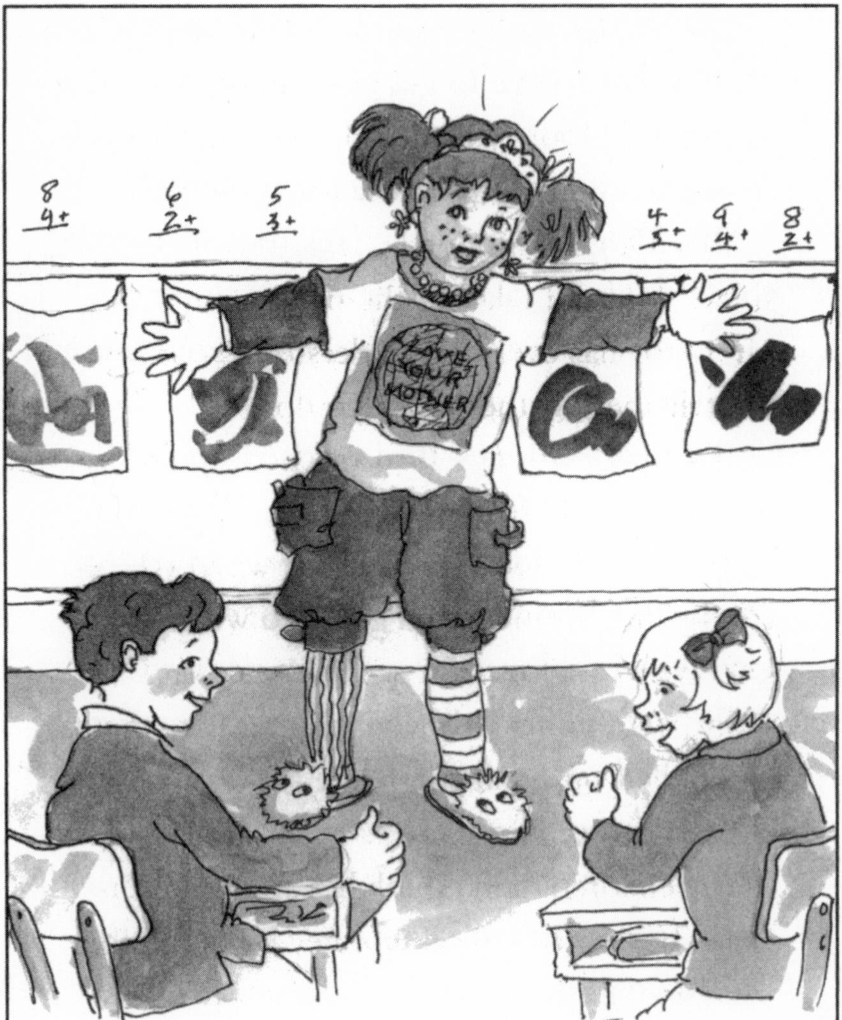
LOVE YOUR MOTHER

"*Très Chic!*" the second-graders all said loudly.

"Good. May I take Mr. Leroy a heart?" she asked. Mrs. Pidgeon held out the small bag of candies, and Gooney Bird selected one. "*U Da Man,*" she read. "He'll like that. I'll be right back," she said.

At the door she looked back and added, "William Henry Harrison never once in his life snowboarded or surfed or wore mouse ears. Moment of silence."

The class became quiet. They could hear the door open and close as Gooney Bird headed out on her visit to the principal.

"Mr. Leroy says yes!" Gooney Bird announced when she returned. Carefully she removed her gloves, folded them neatly, and put them back into her cubby. "He is definitely *Da Man.*"

"Yay!" the children all called. "Awesome!" They clapped and cheered. Then Barry Tuckerman asked, "What did he say yes to?"

"He donated a piece of land to us," Gooney Bird said, "at my request."

"A piece of land?" asked Mrs. Pidgeon.

"Yes. You know that corner of the playground where in good weather there's a seesaw but they take it down for winter?"

Mrs. Pidgeon nodded. She looked through the window. "My goodness! There's Mr. Furillo out there! What's he doing?"

All of the children began to stand up. They wanted to see what the school custodian was doing. Ordinarily he was inside the building, emptying the trash cans, mopping the halls (sometimes he had to clean up throwup, usually in the kindergarten, but he said he didn't mind), and fixing broken things such as pencil sharpeners and towel dispensers.

"Stay seated, children," Mrs. Pidgeon said. She shaded her eyes against the sun with one hand and peered through the window. "It's all packed snow out there. I'm glad he has his warm boots on. He seems to have something in his hand, like a spray can? Yes. A spray can of paint! He's painting a line on the snow!"

"Our borders!" Gooney Bird explained. "Inside that line is our territory. Mr. Leroy donated it to us until vacation."

"But what's it *for*, Gooney Bird?" asked Mrs. Pidgeon.

Gooney Bird hummed a melody very loudly.

"'This Land Is Your Land'!" called Chelsea, recognizing the tune.

"You got it!" said Gooney Bird. "We're going to make us a map from California to the New York island!"

"How?" several children asked. "It's all snowy out there!"

"Ever made sculpture out of sand, on the beach?"

They all nodded. "Sandcastles," Keiko said.

"I built a monster once," Nicholas said, "with tentacles."

"Well, this will be like that, only out of snow," Gooney Bird explained.

"Well! This sounds exciting! Outdoor clothes, everyone!" Mrs. Pidgeon announced.

The children moved toward the hooks that held their jackets.

"Mrs. Pidgeon?" Gooney Bird asked. "Could you bring a map? I know the pull-down one is too big. But do you maybe have a book with a USA map in it?"

"Oh, yes, I'm sure I do." Mrs. Pidgeon went to the bookcase.

"Good. Bring that. And, everybody?" Gooney Bird added, pulling on her boots. "Be prepared to tell us your vacation plans. Every single one of you. Even you, Malcolm." Malcolm scowled.

"Why?" asked Keiko as she wrapped her pink scarf around her neck.

"Because we're going to put us all on the map!"

4.

"Don't get too close or wag your tail, Bruno, until the paint dries," Mr. Furillo warned his dog. The big Newfoundland was watching as the custodian finished drawing the spray-paint line around the huge rectangle of snow-packed playground.

"It wouldn't matter, Mr. Furillo," Nicholas said as the children approached the corner of the playground that Mr. Leroy had given them for the project. "The paint is black, and Bruno's tail is black. It wouldn't even show."

"Ah, but he'd use his tail as a paintbrush,"

Mr. Furillo explained. "He'd paint the halls inside the school!"

Fortunately, Bruno was very obedient, and very lazy. He simply lay down on the snow, his tail tucked under him, and watched while the custodian finished the last line. Mrs. Pidgeon and the children watched, too. "There you are!" Mr. Furillo said. "There's your official territory, all marked off. What do you think? Like it? Need anything else?"

"One more thing," Gooney Bird told him. "Is there still paint in the can?"

He shook it and listened. "Yep. Lots."

"Okay," Gooney Bird told him. "In this corner"—she pointed to the lower right corner of the huge rectangle—"could you make a big plus sign?"

"A plus sign?"

"Yes. You know what that looks like. Two plus two?"

"It's like the 'add' key on a calculator," Barry explained to him.

45

"Oh! Got it!" Mr. Furillo said. "Where do you want it? Right here okay?" he stood in the corner that Gooney Bird had pointed to. She nodded, and he sprayed carefully.

"Oops," he said. "A little wobbly."

"That's all right," Gooney Bird reassured him. "Now we need a letter at each of the four points. N, E, S, W. Can you do that? The N goes at the top."

Mr. Furillo gazed at the plus sign, thinking. "I get it!" he said. "North, east, south, west!"

"Good for you, Mr. Furillo. That's exactly right."

Carefully he sprayed the letters onto the

snow. The children all watched with interest. Bruno snored slightly.

Mr. Furillo stood back and looked. Bruno yawned, got up, stood beside him, yawned, and looked. Mrs. Pidgeon and all of the second-graders looked.

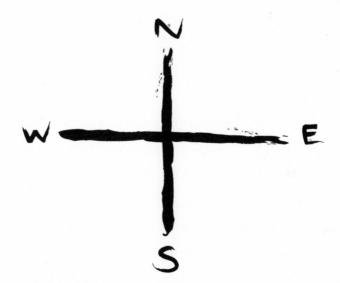

Everyone smiled.

"It's a real map!" Ben said.

"We're going to make a map of the United States inside our territory," Gooney Bird explained.

"I think I'm standing on Antarctica!" Barry Tuckerman said proudly, looking down at his own boots where they were planted on a mound of snow at the lower edge of the marked-off area.

"May I make a suggestion?" Mrs. Pidgeon asked.

"Of course," said Gooney Bird.

"I think," Mrs. Pidgeon suggested, "that if Mr. Furillo sprayed a little arrowhead at the tip of each—"

"Gotcha!" Mr. Furillo said, and he went to work.

"Perfect! May we keep the paint can?" Gooney Bird asked Mr. Furillo. "Once we build our map, we might need to paint the borders."

Mr. Furillo hesitated. "Tell you what. How about if you tell me when you're ready and I'll spray the borders for you?" he asked. "I'll just wait over here."

"Yes, I think it's a good idea if Mr. Furillo is in charge of the spray paint," Mrs. Pidgeon said.

Gooney Bird agreed. "Okay," she said.

Mr. Furillo leaned against the playground fence and Bruno sat beside him. They watched while Mrs. Pidgeon, consulting the map in her book, used a ruler to carefully gouge the outline of a huge United States into the packed snow.

"Florida should be a little longer!" Beanie called. Mrs. Pidgeon looked again at the map, nodded, and lengthened Florida.

"Don't forget that we need the Hawaiian Islands!" Barry said loudly, pointing to the left-hand side of the map. "You can put them over there, out in the Pacific Ocean!"

Mrs. Pidgeon had finished the coast of California with her ruler, and now she stabbed out little circles to make Hawaii.

Ben was examining the top of the map. "See where Maine pokes up?" he said to the teacher. "You did a good job on Maine. But over there, you need a straighter line for the top of Vermont."

Mrs. Pidgeon examined the northeast United States, consulted the map, and sliced a straighter line where Ben was pointing.

Then she looked carefully at the map she had carved from the snow. "Gooney Bird? Everybody? What do you think?" She passed the geography book around. One by one the children compared the pictured map with the snow map. They nodded their heads.

"Excellent, Mrs. Pidgeon!" Gooney Bird said. "Good job!"

"*U Go, Girl*!" Keiko said with a giggle.

"Your turn, Mr. Furillo," Gooney Bird told the custodian. "You can spray the outline now."

"Be really, really careful on Hawaii," Barry said nervously. "It's quite small."

Mr. Furillo shook the paint can hard for a minute. "Stand back, everyone!" he said. "I don't want to get paint on anyone's boots!"

The children, and Mrs. Pidgeon, all retreated to the edge of the territory, to the mound that they called Antarctica, and watched while Mr. Furillo carefully outlined the entire United States in black paint. Then he shook the can again and did Hawaii.

When he was finished, he took a bow, and the children clapped.

"Alaska?" Mr. Furillo asked.

The children shook their heads. They didn't need Alaska.

"Look!" Keiko said, suddenly. She pointed to the building. There were faces in every window of the small school. "Everybody's watching!"

"Mrs. Pidgeon! Mrs. Pidgeon!" said Felicia Ann in a worried voice. "It's almost recess time. All the kids will be coming out. What if everybody steps on our map and wrecks it?"

"They won't," Gooney Bird told her. "Mr. Leroy promised that while we were out here starting our map, he'd get on the intercom and make an announcement about it. Nobody's allowed on this part of the playground except us—the second grade. But when it's all done, then we'll share it with the whole school."

Tyrone began to dance. *"Gonna do a rap,"* he chanted, *"about the playground map!"*

"About the playground map!" the other children repeated.

"Lets dance around the USA!" Malcolm called.

Some of the children danced across the map while Tyrone chanted, *"This map be so cool, we be famous in our school!"* Mr. Furillo, Mrs. Pidgeon, and Bruno watched from Antarctica.

"Famous in our school!" the children repeated.

Finally the line of dancers stopped, and Mr. Furillo said, "Okay. I'm heading back inside. Mrs. Clancy has a loose shelf that needs fixing, in the library. Call me if you need me. C'mon, Bruno!" He waited while the dog lifted his leg over Antarctica briefly, and then they returned to the school.

The second-graders heard the recess bell ring from inside the building. Soon the school doors opened and all of the other children came noisily through.

Mr. Leroy was among them. He was carrying something.

Mrs. Pidgeon and the students watched as the principal came to the edge of the map. With a hammer, he planted a sign which he had hastily made:

2ND GRADE PROJECT

NO TRESPASSING!

A tall fifth-grader named Marlon Washington, who always said that George Washington was his grandfather, but everyone knew he was making it up, came and stood by the sign. He peered at the territory, the map, and its sprayed border. "What's going on?" he asked.

"Secret project," Mr. Leroy explained. "I announced it over the intercom, remember? Just a few minutes ago. The second grade will share it with everyone when it's finished."

"*U Da Man,* Mr. Leroy!" Malcolm shouted.

Marlon Washington looked the situation over. He looked at the map, at the Hawaiian Islands, and at the NESW in the lower right-hand corner. Then he said: "Just a big mess, that's all." He turned and went to play with his classmates in another part of the playground.

Mr. Leroy bowed to the second-graders. "I am *Da Man,*" he said. Then he went back to the school.

"Gather round," Gooney Bird told her classmates. They clustered around her.

"Is anyone here going to Alaska during our winter vacation? Raise your hand if you are."

No hands went up.

"Anyone going to Europe? Asia? China, or Japan?"

No hands. Keiko sighed. "I wish I could," she said. "Maybe next summer."

"India? Australia? Africa?"

No one.

"Okay, then. We don't need to think about those places, at least for now. It was enough work to make the USA and part of South America and then to put Hawaii out there in the ocean. I think we did a great job."

"Gooney Bird?" Barry Tuckerman, standing near Hawaii, waved his mittened hand in the air.

"Yes?"

"What exactly are we going to do with this map?"

"Barry, Barry, Barry," Gooney Bird said, shaking her head at him. "It's not necessary to do something all the time! Sometimes it's enough just to *be!*"

"We could just stand around and admire the map," Felicia Ann suggested in her quiet voice.

"We could hold hands in a circle and sing 'This Land Is Your Land,'" Keiko murmured.

"Hey! We could call the TV station and they could put us on the news!" Tyrone said. "They could bring their camera guy and he could interview me! *Doan wanna cause no flap, but you oughta see our map . . .*" Tyrone began to wiggle his hips. "This here map could make us famous!"

"If they did that," Beanie said, glancing toward Florida, "maybe they could interview us about our vacations. Maybe I could even wear mouse ears during the interv—"

"I could demonstrate my snowboard technique!" Ben interrupted, planting his feet in snowboard position.

"I could bring a ukulele! That's how they play

Hawaiian music, on a ukulele!" Barry began to strum an imaginary instrument.

"ENOUGH!" Mrs. Pidgeon said in a loud, exasperated voice. Then she apologized. "Sorry to shout. But, really, I am so tired of hearing about glamorous vacations. And it's time to go inside. We still have math to do. We have a great start on this map now, and we'll figure out how to proceed. I'm sure Gooney Bird will have some wonderful ideas. She always does."

"Yes. I do," Gooney Bird replied. "Or at least I *will*. I need time to think." She adjusted her multicolored hat and grinned.

5.

"We need ocean," Barry Tuckerman said when they were back in the classroom and looking down on their project from the second grade windows.

"*Yeah,*" chanted Tyrone. "*Don't cause no commotion, but we gotta have a ocean . . .*"

"*Need a magic potion,*" Chelsea continued, giggling, "*to make us have a ocean . . .*"

Mrs. Pidgeon quickly went to the piano and played the chord that usually reminded the children to settle down. "I don't think we need a rap right now, Tyrone," she said. "But I agree that we need an ocean. And by the way, it's *an* ocean, *Cool Dude,* not *a* ocean."

"I know that," Tyrone said with a grin. "Raps don't follow the rules."

Gooney Bird was on tiptoes, her nose pressed against the window. "You know how you're always telling us that we don't need to color inside the lines, Mrs. Pidgeon? That true creative artists don't squinch their colors into outlines?"

"And that's why our art is so good!" Tricia announced. All of the children looked proudly at the colorful paintings that were on the walls around the classroom. "When my mom came for a conference and saw our paintings, she said that our classroom was better than the Museum of Modern Art!"

"It *is!*" Barry announced.

"Yes, it is," Gooney Bird agreed. "But right now we need to make ocean. And it needs to be blue. Can we use our poster paint, Mrs.

Pidgeon? If we mix up a bucket of blue paint and water, Mr. Furillo could use his big sweeping brush and we'd tell him he has to stay in the lines—"

"Yeah, 'cause this isn't *art!* This is a *map!*" Malcolm said.

"Yes, maps are scientific," Nicholas said. "Not creative art."

"Right!" Chelsea said.

"Let's do it!" Mrs. Pidgeon said. She went to the supply closet. "I'll mix up a bucket of paint, and if Mr. Furillo paints the ocean— Gooney Bird, could you go find him in the library and tell him we need him for one more little job?—it will probably freeze tonight. The weather forecast on the radio says it's going to be quite cold. So tomorrow we'll have a good solid ocean around our United States . . ."

"Two oceans!" Malcolm pointed out.

"An Atlantic!" said Tricia.

"And a Pacific!" Chelsea added.

"Oh, dear. I'm worried about something," Keiko said in her small, worried voice.

Gooney Bird was about to leave the room. She turned back at the door. "What are you worried about, Keiko?" she asked. "Something I should mention to Mr. Furillo?"

Keiko nodded. She looked embarrassed. "Bruno," she whispered. "I'm scared—"

"Oh, *Sweet Thing*," Mrs. Pidgeon said. She set down the jar of blue paint and put her arm over Keiko's shoulder. "Bruno is the nicest dog in the world. You've never been nervous around him before. Remember, he marched in our Thanksgiving parade?"

"And he wore fake antlers at our holiday party!" Chelsea reminded Keiko.

"I'm not scared of Bruno," Keiko said. "I *like* Bruno!"

"What's worrying you, then, *Sweet Thing*?" asked Mrs. Pidgeon, looking puzzled.

"He peed on Antarctica," Keiko whispered. "I'm scared he'll ruin our ocean."

"Yeah, I saw him do that," Ben said. "He peed about six gallons."

"My dog's *little*," Barry said. "My dog only pees *one* gallon."

"My triplets," Malcolm began, "pee—"

Mrs. Pidgeon interrupted him. "Math problem! Subtraction!" she announced. "How many more gallons does Bruno—"

"Five!" all the children said together. "That's too easy!"

"Yes, it was, wasn't it?" Mrs. Pidgeon sighed. "But we do need to remember to do our math. We'll work on it while we get the ocean painted. Gooney Bird, could you mention the Bruno problem to Mr. Furillo?"

"I'm on my way," Gooney Bird said. "Start mixing the paint." She saluted. "Oh, also, could I give Mr. Furillo a valentine heart?"

Mrs. Pidgeon held out the bag and Gooney Bird reached in. "Perfect!" said Gooney Bird. "It says *Puppy Love*!" She hurried off to find the custodian.

By the time school ended for the day, and the children were heading for the buses, Mr. Furillo had painted the oceans. Already the temperature was dropping, and the new pale blue had begun to freeze into a shiny crust around North America. Bruno had been told firmly that he must not approach the map. He could lie down on Antarctica if he wanted. He could pee on Antarctica if he wanted. But not on the United States. That included Hawaii.

For homework, each child was taking home a rolled-up map of the United States. They were each to locate where they would be spending their February vacation.

Malcolm was sulking. He said he didn't even want to take his map home. He said he might *burn* his map. He might let the triplets chew on it. He might make a huge paper airplane out of it. He might use it for origami and make an enormous cootie-catcher. He might . . .

He was still grumbling loudly when he boarded his bus.

Gooney Bird, who was a walker, called toward Malcolm's bus as its door hissed closed.

"William Henry Harrison never even *had* a map when he was eight years old!" she said. "Moment of silence!"

But through the bus window she could see that Malcolm wasn't listening. He was using his rolled-up map as a weapon and had begun a swordfight with a fifth-grader, who was stabbing back at him with a ruler. The driver, a gray-haired woman, got up from her seat with an impatient look and went down the aisle to separate the two boys before she began to drive.

Bruno yawned and lay down with his tail end on Antarctica and his head very, very close to the border but obediently not touching the map. While Mr. Furillo put a few pale blue finishing touches on the Pacific Ocean near Hawaii, and the yellow school buses left the driveway one by one, Bruno slept.

6.

The next morning, the entire school was talking admiringly about the second-graders' playground snow map. Overnight the Pacific and Atlantic oceans had frozen into shimmery blue. The United States was a lovely vast landmass, and Mrs. Pidgeon, in doing the outline, had even shoved some snow to create a ridge down the center, where the Rocky Mountains would be.

Hawaii was tiny hard bumps of snow out in the Pacific, and a plastic palm tree from the turtle bowl in the classroom was now wedged onto it. Humphrey the turtle had died in October, and the children had never gotten around to creating a memorial for him. They felt, now, that Humphrey would be proud to be part of Hawaii.

"Moment of silence for Humphrey," Gooney Bird announced, and they all stood reverently for a brief period, staring at the palm tree and remembering what a happy life Humphrey had had in his plastic bowl with its small island until he got the mysterious fungus that had ended it all.

"I brought this," Ben announced, and showed them the small artificial snow-covered pine tree that he'd taken out of his backpack. "It's from my train set."

"What's it for?" asked Malcolm.

"Well, I thought I'd put it in Vermont. There are a whole lot of pine trees there. I'm going to be snowboarding down trails that wind in and out among a zillion pine trees. So . . ." Ben stepped over the border of the second grade territory, walked carefully up into the Atlantic

Ocean, crossed onto land at New York, and began to head north with his little tree.

"Wait!" Gooney Bird commanded, and Ben stopped where he was, with one foot in Connecticut and the other in New York State.

"What?" he asked.

"We have a beautiful map here, and I think it cheapens it to set up this fake plastic stuff. If you put your tree in Vermont, then next I bet anything Beanie will—" She glanced over at Beanie, who had already taken something out of her jacket pocket.

"Hold it up, Bean," Gooney Bird said with a sigh.

Beanie held up a Mickey Mouse with long thin black legs and huge white feet. "It's not plastic; it's rubber," she said defensively.

"It's junky," Chelsea said, wrinkling her nose.

"If we let Ben stand his tree in Vermont," Gooney Bird said, "and Beanie put her rubber mouse in Florida, then everyone will bring some vacation thing, and—let's see, we can make a math problem here . . ."

"Good point, Gooney Bird. Eleven second-graders," Mrs. Pidgeon said, "plus me, because I'm part of this class. That makes twelve. And if three people—Barry, Beanie, and Ben—have already put their, ah, vacation objects down, how many more vacation souvenirs—"

"—will it take to ruin our beautiful map?" Chelsea said.

"Twelve minus three!" shouted Malcolm.

"NINE!"

"It would be a mess. Let's not do it," Tricia said.

"Can we leave the palm tree?" Barry asked.

"Yes," Gooney Bird said. "In memory of Humphrey."

"In memory of Humphrey," all of the children said mournfully.

"Well, all right." Ben reluctantly returned his little pine tree to his backpack. Beanie sighed and folded her rubbery mouse so that he would fit in her pocket again.

"Instead," Gooney Bird explained, "we're going to do something that will be very tasteful and appropriate and artistic and unusual. And also educational.

"Keiko," she asked, "did you bring the special things that I asked you for?"

Keiko nodded happily. "Yes, they're all in my cubby."

"Okay, guys," Gooney Bird said. "Back to the classroom. We have work to do."

"Eleven pairs of mittens equals how many individual mittens?" asked Mrs. Pidgeon as the children hung up their outdoor things. She was still trying to get some math done.

"Twenty-two," Barry said. He was faster than anyone at math.

"Right! Good, Barry. Now, if four children lost their mittens—"

"Lost just one, or the whole pair?" Tricia asked. She draped her knitted scarf over its hook.

"Well, just one. Let's say four mittens had been lost. So how many mittens would remain, out of the twenty-two?"

"I lost both of my mittens at the Harry Potter movie," Nicholas said. "They fell under the seat. And my mom called the theater, but they didn't have them, so my mom thinks someone stole them!"

"Those weren't mittens, Nicholas," Malcolm said. "Those were *gloves* you lost. Those were your Spider-Man gloves!"

"Yeah, and somebody *stole* them! Now look what I have to wear—these dumb baby mittens!" Nicholas glared at the blue knitted mittens he had just put into his cubby.

"Back to our math problem, children!" Mrs. Pidgeon said. "Twenty-two minus four?"

"What if an octopus had mittens?" Malcolm shouted. "It would have *eight!*"

"Octopuses don't have hands," Ben said.

"It's *octopi*," Barry reminded him.

Chelsea went over to where Mrs. Pidgeon was standing. *"U Go, Girl,"* she whispered.

Mrs. Pidgeon, whose shoulders had begun to slump, straightened herself, went to the piano, and played a loud chord. When everyone had fallen silent, she said firmly, "Twenty-two minus four?"

"Eighteen!" the second-graders replied.

"Correct! Good job! Everyone in your seats now, please!"

"Lost your mittens? You naughty kittens!" Tyrone sang as he went to his desk.

"That's a baby song!" Malcolm told him.

Tyrone poked Malcolm in the shoulder as he sauntered past. "So? Who cares? I'm a *Cool Dude!*"

"Mrs. Pidgeon! Mrs. Pidgeon! Tyrone hit Malcolm!" Tricia called.

"Tyrone, sit down *now.* Malcolm? You are a *Class Act*, remember? So let's behave like one."

Malcolm scowled. So did Tyrone. But they both remained silent.

"Go ahead, Gooney Bird," Mrs. Pidgeon said when all of the children were seated and waiting.

Gooney Bird went to the front of the classroom. "All right, Keiko, *Sweet Thing,* pass them out," she said.

Keiko had taken a package wrapped in brown paper from her cubby. Carefully she removed the paper. "My uncle gave me these," she explained. "They came from his restaurant."

"Those are chopsticks!" Malcolm announced, recognizing the narrow wooden sticks. "Are we going to eat Chinese food? Are you going to make us eat rice? I *hate* rice!"

Mrs. Pidgeon went to Malcolm and placed her calm-down hand on his shoulder.

"No Chinese food," Gooney Bird explained.

"These are going to be our flagpoles. You can pass them out, Keiko. One for each person."

Carefully Keiko distributed the chopsticks.

"NO SWORDFIGHTING!" Gooney Bird commanded when she saw Malcolm and Nicholas beginning to aim their chopsticks.

"Next, you each get some construction paper. Sorry, Mrs. Pidgeon, but we're going to make a mess again. You can each choose the color you want." Gooney Bird walked around the desk and waited while each child chose a colored sheet of paper.

"We're each going to cut a rectangle just big enough for a flag at the top of our flagpole. Not yet, Malcolm! Wait!" Malcolm had pulled his scissors out of his desk and was ready to begin cutting a rectangle of dark blue construction paper.

"But we have to be sure that the flag is just big enough for this!" Gooney Bird picked up a small stack of photographs from Mrs. Pidgeon's desk. She held up the top one, a small school photo of Felicia Ann, grinning, with her top teeth missing.

"I'll give you each your own photo, and you'll paste it onto your flag. Carefully cut out your face so that it just fits on your flag, okay?"

The children nodded. They had all gotten their scissors out.

"You too, Mrs. Pidgeon. You'll have a flag, too." Gooney Bird handed the teacher her photograph.

Mrs. Pidgeon looked at it and made a face. "My hair looked awful that day," she said.

"When your flag is done, with the picture on it, then we'll use the stapler to attach it to the flagpole," Gooney Bird explained. "I've already tested this. See?" She held up her own flag. Her chopstick had a purple rectangle attached to it, with Gooney Bird's picture carefully glued to the purple. "My hair looked awful that day too, Mrs. Pidgeon," she said. "I had a bad case of hat hair.

"Okay, start cutting out your faces, and your flags. Mrs. Pidgeon will come around with paste, and then we'll do the stapling really carefully. And be sure to put your flag on the square end! We need the pointy end to stick into the snow."

Chelsea looked up from her photograph, from which she was carefully cutting out her head. "Where are we going to stick them?"

"We'll each plant our flag at the place where we'll be spending our vacation! Barry? *Whiz Kid*? Yours will be right beside Humphrey's palm tree!"

"YES!" said Barry.

The class became very quiet. Everyone, including Mrs. Pidgeon, was carefully creating a flag.

7.

Toward the end of the day, the playground was empty. Two crows sat on the limb of a bare tree and watched as the class, each person carrying a flag, made their way to the snow map. One of the crows made a cawing sound as if he were annoyed at the interruption. Then he and his partner lifted their large wings and flew away.

"Look! A piece of Humphrey's palm tree broke off! Hawaii's all messed up!"

"I bet a bear walked through and broke it while we were having lunch," Tricia said.

"Really?" asked Keiko nervously. "A bear?"

"No, *Sweet Thing*," Gooney Bird reassured her. "I think those crows snapped it off. They're probably looking for nest material."

"Let's get started, class!" Mrs. Pidgeon suggested. "We'll use up all our time just talking and our feet will get cold. How shall we do this, Gooney Bird? Who'll go first?"

Gooney Bird thought for a moment. "Alphabetical," she decided.

"Yay!" Barry shouted. "I always go first alphabetically!"

"I always go last," Tyrone said with a pout.

Felicia Ann went shyly over to Tyrone. *"It maybe be a blast, when you always goin' last,"* she said to him, softly, and Tyrone's face brightened.

"Run my engine pretty fast, 'cuz I be always goin' last," he replied with a grin.

"Cool Dude," Felicia Ann added.

Barry plunged his chopstick in the snow beside the broken palm tree. "Ta-da!" he said. "Hawaii for *Whiz Kid*!" He wiggled his hips in a brief hula.

"Okay. Who's next?" asked Mrs. Pidgeon. "Let me think. Barry, Beanie, Ben, Chelsea . . ."

"Beanie!" Gooney Bird called. "You next, *Sunshine*!"

Beanie, carrying the little flag with her photograph on it, stepped forward onto the map and found Florida. "M-I-C-K-E-Y!" She sang the letters. "M-O-U-S-E!" She leaned down and poked her flag into the snow in the center of Florida.

"Ha! Barry and Beanie both get really bad sunburns," Malcolm said loudly, "and Beanie, she has to wear stupid mouse ears!" Mrs. Pidgeon put her hand gently on Malcolm's shoulder.

"Do you think William Henry Harrison used sunscreen at the beach?" Keiko asked in a curious voice.

"William Henry Harrison never even *went* to the beach, poor guy," Gooney Bird said.

Without any announcement from Gooney Bird, the second grade observed a moment of silence. Poor President Harrison.

Ben went next. He was well prepared, because his family had been planning their ski trip for a long time. Ben knew exactly how to find Sugarbush, Vermont, on their packed-snow map.

"There," he said, after he had poked his flagpole into the snow. "If I had a lot of flags, I could make it look like a slalom course! Whoosh whoosh whoosh, this is me, snowboarding down between the flags! That's what I'm gonna be doing on vacation! *In Style!*"

"I bet you fall and break your leg," muttered Malcolm.

"Snowboard down the slope, and you actin' like a dope . . . " Tyrone chanted.

"Chelsea?" said Gooney Bird. "You're next!"

Chelsea, holding her flag, moved forward slightly onto the map. She started toward California. Then she stopped, and hung her head.

"What's wrong, *QT*?" asked Mrs. Pidgeon.

"Nothing."

"Don't you want to plant your flag?"

But Chelsea shook her head. "I asked my mom if we could go to California during our school vacation. But she said not unless we win the lottery." She looked up. "She said we could go to the pizza place one night, though."

"I see. Well, the pizza place sounds like fun."

"Not as much fun as Hawaii!" shouted Barry.

"Or Disney World!" called Beanie.

"Or Sugarbush, Vermont!" said Ben in a loud voice.

Chelsea began to cry.

Mrs. Pidgeon put her arm around Chelsea. She looked around. "Felicia Ann?" she said. "You're next in the alphabet. *What's Up?*"

"I'm going to the public library," Felicia Ann said in a very small voice.

"Well, that's always exciting," Mrs. Pidgeon said. She glared at Barry, Beanie, and Ben. "Anyone want to go next? Anyone else got a vacation spot to show us?"

One by one the children shook their heads. "I'm going to my grandma's," Nicholas said, "but it's just down the street. Really *Magic. NOT!*"

"I'm going to the movies," Tyrone said. "My dad said he'd take me."

"Cool Dude," muttered Malcolm.

"Keiko?" Mrs. Pidgeon suggested. "How about you, *Sweet Thing?*"

But Keiko said no. "I'm not going anyplace. I'm going to help in my parents' store during vacation."

"Do you get to do the cash register?" Malcolm asked.

"No. But I arrange the fruit. I can make a really beautiful pyramid out of oranges."

"Oh, lovely, Keiko," Mrs. Pidgeon said. "Anyone else? Who has a vacation destination?"

"Not me."

"Not me."

"We're not going anywhere *ever again,*" Malcolm complained, "because of the triplets."

"I'm not going anywhere either," Mrs. Pidgeon said. "I promised my husband I'd spend the vacation finishing a sweater that I started knitting for him in 2004."

"U Go, Girl," Tyrone said, and high-fived the teacher.

"Gooney Bird?" Mrs. Pidegon asked. "What about you? This was your idea."

"And it was a pretty good one," Gooney Bird said in a tentative voice. "We learned a lot about maps."

"But where are you going for vacation, Gooney Bird? Someplace *Très Chic*?" asked Felicia Ann.

Gooney Bird sighed. "I'm staying home," she confessed. "I'm planning to write a novel."

Everyone stared at the big snow-packed map and its three chopstick flagpoles in Hawaii, Vermont, and Florida. They looked very small and far apart.

"We could make a math problem out of this," Mrs. Pidgeon suggested. "If there are twelve people, and three of them go off on a vacation, then how many are left?"

No one said anything. Finally Keiko murmured, "Nine."

"If we put our nine flags here, in this town, it would look like a porcupine sitting on the map," Chelsea observed glumly.

"I have an idea," Barry announced. "How about a moment of silence for everybody in this whole second grade except for me . . . "

"And me!" Beanie said with a grin.

"AND ME!" Ben shouted.

Everyone was very silent. Felicia Ann sniffled quietly and wiped her nose on her sleeve.

"My feet are cold," Nicholas said, after a moment.

"Well," Mrs. Pidgeon suggested. "Let's go inside and regroup."

8.

Inside the classroom, with their outdoor jackets hanging up again and their boots standing in pairs by their cubbies, the second-graders took their seats glumly. Their map project had not been the success they had hoped it would be.

"What're we going to tell the other kids?" Nicholas asked.

"Yes," said Ben, "what about Marlon Washington? He said our project was just a big mess, and we said just wait till it's done! But now he's going to say it's *really* just a big mess!"

Mrs. Pidgeon glanced through the window, down to the playground where the map was.

"The oceans are so blue and beautiful," she said with a sigh. "We really did make a wonderful map. Surely we can think of some educational way to use it.

"Barry?" she asked. "You're the *Whiz Kid.* Any ideas?"

Barry shook his head.

"I know a card game called 'spit in the ocean'! How about if we all go down and spit in . . ." Malcolm suggested. But his voice trailed off and he didn't even finish his sentence.

"You're really a *Class Act*, Malcolm," Chelsea said, and rolled her eyes.

"So?" Malcolm replied. "You got a better idea, *QT*?"

But Chelsea didn't.

"Well," said Mrs. Pidgeon, "let's get out our math books. Gooney Bird, would you pass around these worksheets?" She handed some papers to Gooney Bird, who stood and began to hand one to each child.

At the rear corner of the room, Gooney Bird stopped, suddenly, and began to look at something on a shelf near the supply closet. "We didn't get worksheets over here!" Ben called.

"Oops, sorry," Gooney Bird said, and passed the rest of the sheets to the students in Ben's group of desks. Then she went back and looked again at the shelf. After a moment, she picked up a maroon cardboard box.

Malcolm's hand shot up. "Mrs. Pidgeon!

Mrs. Pidgeon! Gooney Bird took a puzzle from the puzzle shelf! That's not fair! It's math time! Nobody can do a puzzle during math time!"

Mrs. Pidgeon walked to Malcolm's desk and put her calm-down hand on his shoulder. "Relax, Malcolm," she said. "Gooney?" she asked. "What are you doing?"

Gooney Bird didn't answer. She closed her eyes and stood very still. "I'm thinking," she said. "Excuse me for a moment."

Everyone in the room waited. They all watched Gooney Bird, who had now reached into the pocket of the plaid shirt she was wearing today over her red tights. She removed a pair of glasses and put them on, carefully arranging the silver frames around her ears.

"My vision is perfect," she said. "But I feel that sometimes wearing glasses improves concentration. I got these at the Salvation Army store."

"Can you *see* through them?" Keiko asked, in a concerned voice.

"Blurry," Gooney Bird replied. "But seeing blurry helps me think. Mrs. Pidgeon, may I stand here thinking while the class does the worksheets? I'll do mine at home tonight."

Mrs. Pidgeon considered that. "All right," she decided. "How much time do you need?"

"About four minutes and thirty seconds, I think," Gooney Bird said.

"Very well," said Mrs. Pidgeon, glancing at the clock.

Exactly four minutes and seventeen seconds later, Gooney Bird carefully removed her glasses, folded them, and replaced them in her pocket. Carrying the maroon box, she returned to her desk and sat. She was smiling.

"You have an idea, don't you?" Felicia Ann asked. Then she remembered her own candy-heart name. "*What's Up?*"

Gooney Bird grinned.

"You have an idea about our map?" asked Malcolm.

She nodded.

Mrs. Pidgeon collected the math papers quickly. "Let's hear it!" she said to Gooney Bird.

Gooney Bird opened the box. It was filled with oddly shaped wooden puzzle pieces. "Mrs. Pidgeon," she said, "could you read me the list of class names backwards? I mean alphabetically, from the bottom up?"

"Sure," the teacher said. "I'll just read them from the list on the wall. From the bottom: TYRONE."

Gooney Bird shuffled around in the wooden pieces and took one out. "Here you go, *Cool Dude*," she said, and handed the piece to Tyrone, who looked at it, pumped his fist in the air, and said, "Yes! Texas!"

"TRICIA," Mrs. Pidgeon said.

Tricia reached for the puzzle piece that Gooney Bird gave her. "*Pucker Up!*" she said with a grin, and gave her wooden piece a kiss. "Tennessee!"

"Next: NICHOLAS," Mrs. Pidgeon said.

"Wait a minute," Gooney Bird told her, and held out another piece. "You come next, Mrs. Pidgeon. P for Patsy! *U Go, Girl*!" The teacher examined the puzzle piece Gooney Bird handed her. "Hmm," she said. "Pennsylvania. Thanks!"

Then it was time for Nicholas. "Abracadabra, *Magic*!" said Gooney Bird, and gave him Nebraska. Malcolm got Massachusetts, and Keiko smiled when she looked down and saw Kentucky on her piece. "*What's Up*?" asked Felicia Ann with a giggle, and was given Florida. "Here you go, *QT*," Gooney Bird said to Chelsea next, and presented her with the long narrow wooden piece that was California. Then she placed the maroon jigsaw puzzle box on the top of her desk and looked around the room. "Everyone got a state with an initial that matches yours?" she asked, and the children held up their puzzle pieces. All but three.

"I don't!" called Beanie.

"Neither do I!" Barry said.

"Where's mine?" asked Ben.

"Oops!" Gooney Bird responded. "Let me look in the box again. There are a lot more pieces." She shook it, and the wooden pieces rattled inside. She opened the lid, shuffled the pieces around, removed some, and then said, "Nicholas? Here you are!"

Nicholas came forward and she filled his cupped hands. "He already had Nebaska," Gooney Bird explained. "Now: presto! *Magic!* He has Nevada, New Hampshire, New Jersey, New Mexico, New York, North Carolina, and North Dakota." Nicholas looked astonished at first. Then he grinned and went back to his desk with the stack of puzzle pieces.

"That's not fair!" Ben called loudly.

"Well," said Gooney Bird, "there are more pieces. Let me take another look." She shuffled the remaining pieces around in the box.

"Wow! This guy's really a *Class Act*!" Gooney Bird exclaimed. "Come get yours, Malcolm! Hold out your hands!" Malcolm stood, tripped

over his own untied shoelace briefly, then righted himself, and came to collect the pieces as she named them. "Malcolm already had Massachusetts. Now he gets Maine, Maryland, Michigan, Minnesota, Mississippi, Missouri, and Montana!" Malcolm, who so often looked unhappy, was grinning broadly as he went back to his desk. All of the children clapped and cheered. All but three.

"Where's mine?" called Beanie.

"Here, Chelsea, two more for you!" Gooney went to Chelsea's desk and handed her Colorado and Connecticut.

"EXCUSE ME?" Barry Tuckerman stood up and put his hands on his hips. Gooney Bird ignored him.

"And Keiko? You get Kansas."

"Thank you," Keiko replied politely, as she took the wooden piece shaped like Kansas. "It goes very nicely with Kentucky."

"I WANT ONE!" Ben bellowed.

"Me too!" Beanie said angrily.

"I'm going to tell on you, Gooney Bird!" Barry announced loudly.

"Tell what?" Gooney Bird asked.

"That you cheated! You could have used the *world* puzzle! I could have been, ah, Belgium! Or Bolivia!"

"We don't even *have* a world puzzle, Barry," Chelsea pointed out.

"Well. We *should*," Barry muttered. "I'm gonna complain to the principal. I could be Bulgaria!"

"What is Mr. Leroy's first name, Mrs. Pidgeon?" Gooney Bird asked.

The teacher thought for a moment, trying to remember. "John," she said.

"Oh," said Gooney Bird. "What a shame. No state for him, either. Well, let's have a moment of silence in his honor."

9.

"Before we go outside and work again on our map project," Mrs. Pidgeon directed, "let's all open our dictionaries and look up the word *gloating*." She wrote the word on the board.

"Us too? Me and Beanie and Ben? Even though we didn't get any states?" Barry asked.

"I would say especially you three," Mrs. Pidgeon told him.

All of the second-graders took their dictionaries out of their desks and began to turn the pages. Keiko, who was a very fast reader, raised her hand almost immediately.

"Let's wait until we've all read it silently,"

Mrs. Pidgeon said. She sat at her desk and watched all the second-graders with their heads bent over their dictionaries. After a moment she stood up.

"All right," she said. "Now let's think about *gloating*. It means to feel pretty smug because you're better off than someone else. Maybe you've accomplished something, or you have something, that another person hasn't. And the other person feels bad. Who can think of an example of that?"

Barry shot his hand into the air. "Everybody got a state except me and Beanie and Ben! And Malcolm got about a hundred!"

"Eight," Malcolm said. "I got eight."

"So he was gloating," Barry pointed out. "And Gooney Bird was, too! And she did it on purpose!"

Mrs. Pidgeon looked at Gooney Bird. She tilted her head in a questioning way, and waited.

"It's true," Gooney Bird said. "I did it on purpose. It made you feel bad, didn't it?"

Barry nodded.

"I almost cried," Beanie said. "I bit my lip really hard to keep from crying."

"I'm sorry. It was mean of me. I was getting even," Gooney Bird explained.

"For what?" Ben asked.

"Think back," Mrs. Pidgeon said. "Was there a time, not very long ago, when you and Barry and Beanie realized you had something that the rest of us didn't have? And we all felt pretty sorry for ourselves?"

"No. Never," Ben replied. "We never—"

"Yes, we did, Ben," Beanie interrupted. "It was about our vacations."

"Yes. We gloated," Barry pointed out.

"Gloat, gloat, gloat," Beanie said.

"Oh," Ben said. "I get it."

The class sat silently for a moment. Then Mrs. Pidgeon said, "All right. Let's get ready to work some more on our snow map. I want you all to do some research and find an interesting, little-known fact about your state."

"Can we use the library?" asked Malcolm.

"Of course. That's the best place for research."

"And the computers?" asked Keiko.

"Sure."

"Can I use my lunch box?" asked Tyrone.

All of the children admired Tyrone's lunch box, the one with the map of the United States on it, and a star on each state. Inside each star was the name of a famous person who had been born in that state.

"Hey, Tricia: Dolly Parton was born in Tennessee," Tyrone pointed out. "I don't even need to go look. I got my lunch box memorized."

Mrs. Pidgeon gave that some thought. "You know what?" she said. "I think we should concentrate on history or geography, not celebrities."

"Dolly Parton was born in 1946," Tyrone pointed out. "That's history."

"Ancient history!" Tricia added.

"Nonetheless. Let's not use the lunch box.

That would make things too easy. Let's do some real research and find out little-known facts about our states."

"Beyoncé was born in Texas," Tyrone whispered loudly to Tricia. Mrs. Pidgeon gave him a what-did-I-just-say look, and he raised his arms as if he were surrendering. "Busted," he said, with a grin. "Okay. No lunch box."

"Moment of silence," said Mrs. Pidgeon. "Then we'll get to work."

The second-graders all bowed their heads briefly. All but Beanie, Barry, and Ben. "What about *us?*" they asked angrily. What are *we* supposed to do?"

"Gooney Bird?" said Mrs. Pidgeon.

"Let me think," said Gooney Bird. She arranged her tiara on her head once again. "Okay," she said, after a moment. I have an idea."

10.

The librarian, Mrs. Clancy, was happy to have the second-graders visit the library for their map project. She showed them the books about the United States, and where to find the encyclopedia, and she got some of them started on the computers. Nicholas and Malcolm sat at the same table with the encyclopedia volumes marked N and M.

"Remember," Mrs. Pidgeon instructed them. "One little-known fact! Nothing obvious! We want to surprise people! Are you all finding your states?"

The children nodded.

"Here's New Jersey!" Nicholas said loudly, looking at his volume with a grin. Then, after a minute, turning the pages, he added, "North Dakota!"

"Maine!" Malcolm announced, and then: "Massachusetts! Missouri!"

All around the large library room, children were finding their states.

"I Googled California!" Chelsea called out from her computer desk. "And there's a million different things to look at!"

Beanie, Ben, and Barry sat silently near an exhibit of igloos constructed from sugar cubes. They didn't have any research to do. They had no states. But they didn't look upset anymore. Their job was different. And for now they had to wait.

After a few minutes, Gooney Bird made her way over to them and sat down. "I got my little-known fact about Georgia.

Here—I've written it down for you," she told them, and handed them her paper.

Barry looked at what she had written. Then he grinned. "Okay," he said. "Got it."

Next, Tyrone came to the corner of the library where the three Bs were sitting. "I had Texas," he said. "Here." He gave his paper to Beanie. Barry and Ben looked over Beanie's shoulder and they read the Texas little-known fact together. Then they whispered back and forth, and finally they high-fived each other and said, "YES!"

"We got the best job," Beanie said happily to the other two *B*s.

Barry nodded in agreement. Ben whispered, "Maybe. But let's not gloat."

It took several days for the children to prepare their material and to memorize their parts. They had to learn, too, how to locate their states. Only the outline of the USA was marked on their map. Some states, like Florida and Texas and California, were easy to find. So was Hawaii. But North Carolina? Nebraska? Nicholas had to work hard on those, and his other N states. And Malcolm, though he had no trouble with Maine or Massachusetts, struggled with others of his *M*s: Missouri, Minnesota, and the others.

They didn't rehearse outdoors, with the real map, because they didn't want the other classrooms to see them. They wanted the event to be a surprise. But they practiced and practiced in the classroom. Mrs. Pidgeon pulled down the wall map and one by one each child went to the front of the room, announced a state, located it on the map, and recited a little-known fact in a loud clear voice.

Mrs. Pidgeon did, too. She had Pennsylvania.

The three *B*s, Barry and Beanie and Ben, stood to the side, near the classroom door, and presented *their* part during the rehearsals.

"We have to work harder than everybody else," Barry announced one afternoon when they were all taking a break, "because we have to do every state. Our role is *huge*."

"No gloating, remember?" Malcolm reminded him.

"I wasn't gloating. I was just saying."

Mrs. Pidgeon interrupted them. "Everyone's doing a great job, guys," she said. "I'd say we're just about perfect. And tomorrow's the big day! Last day of school before vacation! The whole school will be gathered out on the playground to watch our performance."

"I'm a little bit nervous," Felicia Ann confessed.

"Think of it as *excited*," Gooney Bird told her. "We're *all* excited."

"I wish we had costumes," Chelsea said with a sigh.

"Costumes are for entertainment," Mrs. Pidgeon pointed out, "like a circus, or a pageant. This is more serious. This is an educational event."

"But hats are always good," Gooney Bird said. "I'm going to wear a very spectacular hat. Maybe you could, too, Chelsea? Maybe *everyone* could."

All of the second-graders nodded. They liked that idea.

"But right now," Gooney Bird added, "I need to go see Mrs. Clancy at the library. So I'm putting on my white gloves." She went to her cubby.

"But we see Mrs. Clancy all the time! You don't need white gloves to see the librarian!" Tricia said, laughing.

But Gooney Bird was already smoothing her gloves over her fingers. "This is an official call," she said. "We need her help with AV."

"That's Arizona and Virginia, right?" Malcolm said.

"Good guess, Malcolm," Gooney Bird told him. "but no. It's audio-visual. Librarians are AV experts. And I think the three *B*s are going to need a microphone tomorrow.

"Be right back!" she said, and went off to the library with the white gloves on her hands.

11.

It was a beautiful sunny afternoon. The huge ice map glistened, its oceans sparkling and blue. The black painted line around the United States was firm and wide, and the tiny green plastic palm tree, one frond missing, stood slightly tilted on a small bump that was meant to be part of Hawaii. The chopstick flagpoles that had once decorated Vermont, Florida, and Hawaii had been removed.

Bruno was sprawled, snoring, a little north of Oregon and Washington. "Bruno's in Alaska," Tricia whispered to Nicholas.

A thick orange electrical cord ran all the way from the slightly opened window of the school office, and was providing the power to an amplifier that looked like a black suitcase set against a snowbank. From the top of the amplifier, another cord stretched to a microphone that was standing beside the low mound of packed snow that the children had named Antarctica. Barry, Beanie, and Ben, wearing matching knitted ski hats, were behind the microphone, looking nervous.

"Testing, testing," Barry said into the mike, following Mrs. Clancy's instructions. "One, two, three, four . . ."

The microphone screeched, and the librarian adjusted the volume knob on the amplifier until the piercing screech disappeared. "All right," she said at last. "I think we're ready."

Watertower Elementary School was very small. There was only one class for each grade, from kindergarten through sixth. All eighty-seven students were gathered in the playground,

facing the large map, with Mrs. Pidgeon's class in the front of the crowd. The second-graders were wiggling with nervousness and excitement.

The principal, Mr. Leroy, went to the edge of the map and faced the audience.

"I am *Da Man*," he announced in a loud voice.

"*U Da Man!*" the children all replied.

"And I am delighted to present to you this amazing project created by the second grade." Mr. Leroy gestured to the map. He nodded to the second-graders, all except the three *B*s, who were still arranged behind the microphone. They moved forward, with Mrs. Pidgeon, as they had rehearsed, in a line and took their places, standing on the wide black rectangular border that marked their territory.

"They have been studying United States geography, and now, before we all head off on our wonderful winter vacations, they are going to tell you some little-known facts about this country of ours. First, shall we all join together and sing 'This Land Is Your Land'?"

Mr. Bornstein, the music teacher, came forward and began the song. The children all joined in. Even the kindergarten children knew the words. "This land is your land, this land is my land," they sang loudly.

Mr. Leroy went back to his place in the audience, and Mrs. Pidgeon stepped forward. "I want to introduce our special trio," she said, and gestured toward the three *B*s. "Barry, Beanie, and Ben are going to provide the sound effects—and perhaps you will all join in—as we tell you all little-known facts about some of the United States.

"I'll go first. My state is Pennsylvania." Mrs. Pidgeon stepped onto the map and found the location of her state. She stood carefully on that spot. "Pennsylvania leads the whole country in the manufacture of pretzels and potato chips!" she announced loudly. Then she looked at the sound-effects trio and nodded.

"CRUNCH!" Barry, Beanie, and Ben said into the microphone. They gestured to the audience, who joined in. "CRUNCH!" everyone shouted, and laughed.

Keiko was next in line. She moved to the map, found her place in the exact center of the United States, stood there proudly, and tried to use her loudest voice. "I could have taken Kentucky, but we decided we'd each just do one state. So I chose Kansas," she said, "because it's where *The Wizard of Oz* was!"

The schoolchildren all murmured and nodded. They all knew *The Wizard of Oz.*

"And here's my little-known fact: Kansas has over fifty tornados every year!"

Keiko looked over at the three *B*s. She nodded.

Barry, Beanie, and Ben each took a deep breath. Then, all together, they made the sound of an approaching tornado. "WHOOSH!"

The audience replied loudly: "WHOOSH!"

Tricia went next. She made her way very carefully across the map, finding her place midway between Mrs. Pidgeon, who was standing in Pennsylvania, and Keiko, in Kansas, and then moving a little south of them both.

The sound-effects trio looked a little nervous.

"I'm Tennessee," Tricia announced proudly. "Home of Elvis Presley!" She nodded to the trio.

"YOU AIN'T NUTHIN' BUT A HOUND DOG!" Barry, Ben, and Beanie sang.

The audience repeated it. "YOU AIN'T NUTHIN' BUT A HOUND DOG!" Bruno opened his eyes, looked up sleepily, and then stood. He yawned, moved from Alaska across the Pacific Ocean, and lay down next to Hawaii.

"Me next?" asked Nicholas, and Gooney Bird nodded. *"Magic,"* she whispered, reminding him of his candy-heart name, because he looked a little nervous.

Nicholas moved to the map and turned to face the audience. "I got a whole bunch of states," he said. "Nebraska, Nevada, New Hampshire, New Jersey. New York, North Carolina, North Dakota"—he examined the map carefully, then stepped onto an area beside Texas— "but I chose New Mexico for a really scary reason!"

The children all waited, wondering what little-known fact could be so scary about New Mexico.

"There are a zillion rattlesnakes in New Mexico!" Nicholas announced.

"HISSSSSS," said the sound-effects trio.

"HISSSSSS," repeated the audience in delight.

Tyrone took his turn next. He pranced from the edge of the map over to Texas, near Nicholas in New Mexico. He wiggled his hips slightly and chanted, *I got Texas as my place, Texas sends us into space!* Then he stopped dancing and said, "Texas has the NASA Space Center!"

The three *B*s leaned toward the microphone and said, "BLAST OFF!"

"BLAST OFF!" came the reply.

Chelsea moved proudly to the map and found her spot in the middle of California. Bruno looked over briefly from the Pacific Ocean, then closed his eyes again.

"My state is California!" Chelsea announced. "I could have had Colorado or Connecticut, but I chose California because the state bird is the California quail, and it makes the sound of a city that isn't even in California. Listen hard!"

The trio had studied this very carefully. They had listened to recorded bird calls on the computer in the library. Now the three of them together, in squeaky, warbling voices, did the call: "CHICAAAHGO, CHICAAAHGO, CHICAAAHGO!"

The audience laughed and tried to do it themselves. "CHICAAAHGO, CHICAAAH-GO, CHICAAAHGO!"

Malcolm, who had been wiggling in anticipation, went to the map next. "Me and Nicholas had more states than anybody! Eight! I had Maryland, Michigan, Massachusetts, Minnesota, Missouri, Montana, and Mississippi, but I chose Maine!"

He went to the farthest north spot on the Eastern Coast and stood there beside the Atlantic Ocean, on the border of Canada.

Usually Malcolm talked very fast when he was nervous or excited. But he had practiced and practiced his little-known fact, and now he said it loudly and clearly. "Maine's lowest recorded temperature is fifty below zero!"

"BRRRR!" was the response from the sound-effects trio.

"BRRRR!" the audience replied.

"Now me, now me!" Felicia Ann scurried over to the lower end of the East Coast. "I'm Florida!" she called. "Florida has more lightning strikes than anyplace else in the United States!"

"ZAP!" said the three *B*s.

"ZAP!" said the audience.

Finally, Gooney Bird moved to the state just above Florida. "I'm last, and my state is Georgia," she explained to the audience. Then she told them, "Not many people know this, but Georgia is the headquarters for Coca-Cola!"

She nodded to the trio. "BURP!" they said into the microphone.

"BURP!" The audience, laughing, responded.

"We hope you've enjoyed our geography presentation," Gooney Bird said to the school. "And we hope you all have a great vacation. Anybody who wants to come to my house next Wednesday afternoon, I'm having a birthday party for President William Henry Harrison. His birthday was February ninth and I feel that he doesn't get enough attention, so I am making cookies with his initials in M&M's and you are all invited."

Gooney Bird bowed. The second-graders, and Mrs. Pidgeon, still standing on their states, bowed. The audience applauded. The yellow school buses had lined up along the curb beside

the playground. People began making their way toward the buses. Mr. Furillo prodded Bruno awake and attached a leash to his collar. Mrs. Clancy unplugged the microphone cord, which gave a final small screech. "Good job, sound-effects people," she said to the three *B*s.

"Thank you," they said, but their voices were unenthusiastic.

"That's no fair," Barry complained as he walked past Gooney Bird. "I have to be in Hawaii! I'll miss your party!"

"Yeah," grumbled Ben, coming up beside them. "My family's making me go to Vermont!"

Beanie plodded past them. "I'm missing all the good stuff," she said in a grouchy voice, "just because of dumb Disney World."

"We'll think of you as we eat our cookies," Gooney Bird told them. "We'll be sad for you. We'll have a moment of silence."

The End

Read more about Gooney Bird in these books by Lois Lowry:

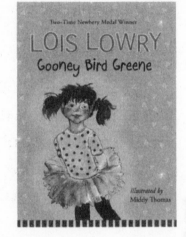